No Bubble, BIG Trouble!

Jodi Rabbow

Written & Published by Jodi Rabbow
Illustrated by Amber Shell & Jodi Rabbow
Designed & Edited by Aspen Ginthum

First U.S. Edition: August 2020.

Library of Congress Cataloging-in-Publication Data

Rabbow, Jodi.
No bubble, big trouble! / Jodi Rabbow. - 1st U.S. edition.
p. cm.
ISBN 978-1-7352080-2-2 (hardcover)
ISBN 978-1-7352080-3-9 (paperback)
ISBN 978-1-7352080-5-3 (eBook)
[1. Fiction. 2. Children's fiction. 3. Self-help techniques.]

10 9 8 7 6 5 4 3 2 1

Dedicated to those who have walked before me, those who walk with me, and those that will follow after me.

Everyday when I wake up, my mom and dad place me in a **big**, **bright**, **shiny** Golden Bubble. It starts at the top of my head and goes all the way down to the bottom of my feet and underneath.

I can feel my Golden Bubble in every direction… **up**, **down**, and **all around**.

Inside my Golden Bubble I feel my **heart**, and I feel **safe**.

My Golden Bubble **protects** me when I feel frightened or scared.

Sometimes, at school on the playground, some of the children are not nice to me.

It makes me sad when people are mean to other people.

I **remember** my Golden Bubble
and put a huge **smile** on my face.

Inside my Golden Bubble I feel the **power** and the **strength** to be me.

I feel like I can use my **voice** and just **be myself**.

My Golden Bubble helps me stay in my own space and feel my own energy.

My grandparents have always said I am **super sensitive**.

When that happens, they **remind** me to go inside my Golden Bubble, and **I feel awesome**.

When I feel overwhelmed or a bit too **sensitive**, my mom reminds me to go **inside** my Golden Bubble.

My Golden Bubble helps me to feel calm, centered, and confident.

I remember my mom placing her hand on my **heart** and **smiling**.

"No bubble, BIG trouble!" my mom says as we both break out into **laughter**. I **love** my Golden Bubble and my **special tools**.

In appreciation for and special thanks to my elders
for all of your love and support.

Made in the USA
Coppell, TX
23 August 2020